Lascivious Something

by Sheila Callaghan

A SAMUEL FRENCH ACTING EDITION

SAMUEL FRENCH

FOUNDED 1830

NEW YORK HOLLYWOOD LONDON TORONTO

SAMUELFRENCH.COM

ISBN 978-0-573-69925-2   Printed in U.S.A.   #29867

MUSIC USE NOTE

Licensees are solely responsible for obtaining formal written permission from copyright owners to use copyrighted music in the performance of this play and are strongly cautioned to do so. If no such permission is obtained by the licensee, then the licensee must use only original music that the licensee owns and controls. Licensees are solely responsible and liable for all music clearances and shall indemnify the copyright owners of the play and their licensing agent, Samuel French, Inc., against any costs, expenses, losses and liabilities arising from the use of music by licensees.

IMPORTANT BILLING AND CREDIT
REQUIREMENTS

All producers of *LASCIVIOUS SOMETHING* must give credit to the Author of the Play in all programs distributed in connection with performances of the Play, and in all instances in which the title of the Play appears for the purposes of advertising, publicizing or otherwise exploiting the Play and/or a production. The name of the Author *must* appear on a separate line on which no other name appears, immediately following the title and must appear in size of type not less than fifty percent of the size of the title type.

In addition the following credit *must* be given in all programs and publicity information distributed in association with this piece:

Originally developed by Cherry Lane Theatre,
Angelina Fiordellisi, Artistic Director

Los Angeles debut produced by Circle X Theater Co. and the
Los Angeles County Arts Commission at [Inside] The Ford,
Hollywood, California

Originally produced in New York City in 2010 by Women's Project, Julie Crosby,
Producing Artistic Director, and Cherry Lane Theatre,
Angelina Fiordellisi, Artistic Director

LASCIVIOUS SOMETHING received its debut production in Los Angeles in March 2010 with Circle X Theatre Co. at [Inside] the Ford. It was produced by Tim Wright and Jennifer A. Skinner. The production was directed by Paul Willis with set design by Sibyl Wickersheimer, lighting design by Thomas Ontiveros, costume design by Dianne K. Graebner, and sound design by John Zalewski. The cast was as follows:

AUGUST	Silas Weir Mitchell
LIZA	Alana Dietze
BOY	Alina Phelan
DAPHNE	Olivia Henry

LASCIVIOUS SOMETHING received its world premiere in New York City in a May 2010 co-production between Women's Project (Julie Crosby, Producing Artistic Director) and Cherry Lane Theatre (Angelina Fiordellisi, Artistic Director). It was originally developed as part of Cherry Lane's 2006 Mentor Project. The co-production was directed by Daniella Topol, with set design by Marsha Ginsberg, costume design by Theresa Squire, lighting by Christopher Akerlind, sound design and original music by Broken Chord Collective. The cast was as follows:

AUGUST	Rob Campbell
LIZA	Dana Eskelson
BOY	Ronete Levenson
DAPHNE	Elisabeth Waterston

CHARACTERS

AUGUST
DAPHNE
LIZA
BOY

AUTHOR'S NOTES

A stroke (/) marks the point of interruption in overlapping dialogue. When the stroke is not immediately followed by text, the next line should occur on the last syllable of the word before the slash – not an overlap but a concise interruption.

The playwright would like to thank the following people, without whose support, guidance, advice, and talents over the years this play would not have been possible:

Amy Mueller, Michael Weller, Mark Christian Subias, Linsay Firman, Eisa Davis, Jason Grote, Rob Handel, Anne Marie Healy, Laramie Dennis, Soho Rep, Daniel Aukin, Kent Nicholson, South Coast Repertory, Jerry Patch, Jennifer Kiger, Jess Bauman, Jay Jennings, Rob Kaplowitz, Jen Carter, Megan Carter, Julie Crosby, Angelina Fiordellisi, Marya Mazor, Jackie Wright, Sophocles Papavasilopoulos, Lia Aprille, Heidi Schreck, Flora Diaz, Mark Subias, Seth Glewen, Suzanne Agins, Charles Borland, Danielle Skraastad, Christina Bennett Lind, Jesse Camp, James King, Sherry Kramer, Darren Pettie, Amy Ryan, Shana Dowdeswell, Chris Kipiniak, Jen Kays, Maria Striar, Kip Fagan, and Deron Bos.

ACT ONE

(**AUGUST** *is a weathered, emaciated, older-than-his age. He's covered in dirt and his fingers are stained red and covered in small cuts.*)

(*He is out in the field, tending his vines.*)

(*It is 1980.*)

AUGUST. My one hand. This hand, with its million minor cuts. Watched it move through the air. Watched it stretch its fingers toward the neck. The middle one trembling like a thin live wire. Curling as they reached the neck, curling around the back, finger finger finger finger thumb, then TOUCH, cool, like everything good in life, you know that kind of cool, and the red inside…the word I want to use is LUSH, red lush like the million minor cuts on my hands…but cooler than blood…

I knew then my life was about to change.

I held it by its neck, I felt its cool. I wondered if my blood would cool with it. I wondered if it could sense my touch somehow, if the atoms spun differently beneath my palm. I stood a respectful distance from it. Gripping. Not gripping, something more respectful than gripping. Because *I* was the one being gripped, you see. So. *Holding,* and I let the air between us fill and fill, with. With. That emotion you reserve only for the most holy of objects.

Brought it upstairs, placing both feet on each step, and allowed it to be taken from my hands just long enough to be placed into my carrier. How much, I heard myself asking. My heart did not race as I thought it would, but I *did* bite my tongue.

AUGUST. *(cont.)* I barely saw the money leaving my fist, damp cash, barely saw the roiling concern in their eyes – they saw my cuts, I suppose, or maybe the worn soles of my sandals – and when the carrier was handed back to me its weight was sweeter than any weight that had *ever* loaded my pockets.

At home…You did WHAT, she said…but I hardly heard her. She was a little naked brown bean on the white sheets while I was plaster and roof and sky and clouds and black space. You did WHAT she said again, but with less conviction…and I realized she was making herself okay with it…The money. Everything.

And then she said. In her smallest, warmest voice. I hope you know what you're doing.

(He regards the bottle and smiles widely.)

A fundamental impossibility. Fuck yeah.

*(**DAPHNE** is seated at a worktable on a porch. She is 24 and poised, striking; a dark flower with a long willowy stem. She wears a work-shirt and jeans.)*

(A modest, aging home sits behind her. She is surrounded by a trellis with grape leaves and bunches of fruit hanging down. She wears a sweater – it is slightly chilly. November in the Mediterranean.)

(She is scraping into a clay block. Every now and then she will consult a photo of the property.)

*(**LIZA** appears. She is also weathered beyond her years, out of breath. She carries a small book and a small bag and wears a large-brimmed hat.)*

LIZA. H-hello, I.

*(**DAPHNE** looks up and smiles. **LIZA** flips through her phrase book.)*

Sorry, *Ya-mas, Keery Moo. / Eethen*

DAPHNE. *(Greek accent – much like Spanish)* I speak your language.

.

LIZA. *(out of breath)* Oh, Super. There's a. Sign actually. TWO signs, but. A man with a donkey. Could I sit?

DAPHNE. Please.

LIZA. Thanks. I'm so winded! Kept thinking I was at the. Summit but then there'd be ANOTHER...so and gosh the donkey had like a beard?

DAPHNE. Ah.

LIZA. So I started up the. Thing again, but the path is all overgrown.

DAPHNE. My husband has been very busy. He means to cut down the wild grasses but it is harvest and we have only one boy full-time.

LIZA. Do you know the donkey I'm talking about?

DAPHNE. You are American?

LIZA. I am. It had a beard. And eyebrows.

DAPHNE. My husband is American. He does not see Americans often. We get British, Germans. Mostly the summer.

LIZA. And the fella was SUCH an excuse me asshole. I think he hates your. I don't know what he hates exactly.

DAPHNE. You say that why?

LIZA. He kept spitting. *Ftou, ftou!* Greek-greek-greek, *ftou!*

DAPHNE. He is short and like a prune.

LIZA. Prune-like, yes, and. Wheew. Angry?

DAPHNE. My husband will come up for his omelet shortly. Will you have some omelet with him?

LIZA. Um. Sure.

DAPHNE. You have arrived on a special day. It is the last day of harvest for the season.

LIZA. Hey! Great!

DAPHNE. How long do you anticipate staying with us?

LIZA. Hadn't figured / actually

DAPHNE. We charge ten American dollars per night, or we have a weekly rate of sixty American dollars.

LIZA. Okay.

(**DAPHNE** *stands and retrieves a decanter filled with wine from the corner. She hands* **LIZA** *a glass and fills it.*)

DAPHNE. Welcome to our Island.

LIZA. Oh, it's...kind of early but what the heck! I'm on VACATION. Salut.

(**LIZA** *raises her glass.*)

You aren't having any?

DAPHNE. No.

LIZA. Okay....

(**LIZA** *drinks deeply from the glass.* **DAPHNE** *returns to her sketching.*)

SWEET.

DAPHNE. It is not good. It is the run-off, so it is fortunate you do not pay so much attention in the sipping.

LIZA. Oh. I never really do. Just sorta knock it back and wait to get. Heh dizzy.

(**DAPHNE** *smiles politely.*)

Boy, you're. Beautiful, I wasn't quite uh prepared...

DAPHNE. Where did you say you heard of us?

LIZA. This hostel in Italy, in Rome actually, and the – I've been traveling, so...and you know there's, they have the the. Corkboards. For backpackers.

DAPHNE. You do not have a backpack.

LIZA. No. Are you from nearby, or.

DAPHNE. My family is a small village a few kilometers away. *From,* is *from.* There are legends here...perhaps you shall hear some.

(**LIZA** *glances around the space and notices a black and white photograph.*)

LIZA. Is this your....

DAPHNE. My husband, yes. Seven years ago.

LIZA. Nice. You took this?

DAPHNE. It was my semester abroad. I studied art. My thesis was a photo essay on the vineyards of the Napa Valley. Months later I brought him here.

LIZA. Why?

(beat)

DAPHNE. It's my family's land.

*(**LIZA** examines the photo.)*

LIZA. What's wrong with his eyes?

*(**DAPHNE** takes the photo from **LIZA**.)*

DAPHNE. It was harvest and he was an apprentice. Picking and pressing and tasting and not sleeping, he was drunk all the time...a piece of twine being frayed very slowly.

(beat)

He believes he is about to revolutionize the entire industry of wine-making. He does nothing small.

*(**LIZA** looks up at the grape vines woven overhead.)*

LIZA. Well I am delighted to be here. To be here in this place, this. Donkeys that need a shave, ha! And such a, an astonishing...It's. You know? HUMBLING. And these, these handsome...

DAPHNE. Help yourself.

LIZA. Don't you need them?

DAPHNE. We do not harvest those. They are for decoration. Please.

LIZA. Oh no no no no no...

*(**DAPHNE** stands and picks a stem of grapes. She feeds one to **LIZA**, slowly.)*

DAPHNE. You will find we are very generous people. Do not hesitate to ask for anything.

LIZA. ...what's your name.

DAPHNE. *(voiced TH, "Thahf'-nee")* Daphne.

LIZA. Th. Oh, DAF-nee. Like in Scooby-Doo.

(**DAPHNE** *smiles.*)

DAPHNE. No. And how do they call you?

(a small beat)

LIZA. Liza.

(**DAPHNE** *maybe registers this.* **LIZA** *shoves the remainder of the grapes into her mouth.*)

(a beat)

As in "Minnelli."

(a beat)

Is there somewhere I could go get cleaned / up

DAPHNE. Of course. The guest house is down those steps and around the back. You are the first door, the suite. The key is in the handle and the sheets are starched and folded for the bed.

LIZA. Super. Thanks.

(**LIZA** *exits.*)

(A beat. **DAPHNE** *realizes she is still holding the photo of* **AUGUST**. *She places it back on the table.*)

(**AUGUST** *sweeps into sight, singing loudly in Greek. He's a little tipsy.*)

AUGUST. *Na ena karidi*
Na ena zoozooni
Fa'eh toh zoozooni prota
Ella hondreh'
(Translation:
"Here's a walnut
Here's a bug
Eat the bug first
Hey fatty")

(He suddenly roars loudly.)

Aftos ine o thorivos pou kratousa mesa mou gia dio meres. (Translation: "That is the sound I have been holding in for two days.")

DAPHNE. *Sigharitiria, agapi mou (Translation:* "Congratulations, agapi-mou.")

AUGUST. Thank you, *kota. Ine i sampania kria. (Translation:* "Is the Champagne chilled?")

DAPHNE. *Ke pote den ine. (Translation:* "When is it not.")

(AUGUST *retrieves a bottle from the cooler and pours himself a glass. She watches him carefully.*)

DAPHNE. *Ehis homa sta hili sou. Pali tros homa… (Translation:* "You have earth on your lip. Eating your dirt again…")

AUGUST. *Matheno pos i gevsi pezi mesa sta stafilia. Kita gia ton eafto sou. (Translation:* "I can taste how it plays into the grapes. See for yourself.")

(*He kisses her.*)

DAPHNE. Ick.

AUGUST. *De tha fas homa.* Woman. *Epidi ise homa.* Filthy filthy chicken… *(Translation:* "You won't eat dirt. Woman. Because you ARE dirt.")

(*He begins to kiss her. She notices his hands covered in cuts.*)

DAPHNE. *Vlepis! Ti krima! (Translation:* "Look! What a pity!")

AUGUST. Ah, scissors broke again. Some reason the stems were so tough this year…

(**DAPHNE** *retrieves a damp rag.*)

DAPHNE. Did Boy throw up?

AUGUST. You should see him down there with the crushers, pressing his little heart out…

DAPHNE. *Afto simeni ne? (Translation:* "That is yes?")

AUGUST. Yes. He threw up. At around five-thirty.

DAPHNE. *Pini para poli sti sigomidi. (Translation:* "He drinks too much during harvest.")

AUGUST. Let him drink as much as he wants, long as it doesn't affect his work…

DAPHNE. *Ase to katharizma gia avrio. Ine methismenos / simera. (Translation:* "Save clean-up for tomorrow. He will be too hung over / today")

AUGUST. He'll do as he's done every other year.

(He touches her tummy.)

Pos estanese? (Translation: "How are you feeling?"*)*

DAPHNE. *Kourasmeni. I naftia me ksipnise. (Translation:* "Tired. The queasy woke me."*)*

(He kisses her, then grabs a rag and begins wiping his hands.)

AUGUST. You know what I was thinking today? How this all suddenly has a purpose. I mean it did before, but. I dunno. This little blastocyst...he's like a, like a root. Connecting us. I get all choked up thinking about it.

DAPHNE. *Avgusto* –

AUGUST. Ow. Weird. My knuckle. When I move my hand like this, my knuckle hurts. See like this, it hurts. Like this, it doesn't. This, ow. This, no. Ow, no. Ow, no.

DAPHNE. *Kapios ine 'tho. (Translation:* "Someone is here."*)*

AUGUST. Here? From the village?

DAPHNE. *Mia Americaneetha. (Translation:* "An American."*)*

AUGUST. That's odd...a tourist?

DAPHNE. Someone from your past.

(a beat)

A woman.

AUGUST. Who?

*(**DAPHNE** does not answer.)*

Daphne...

DAPHNE. The one who bites.

*(**LIZA** enters.)*

LIZA. I had trouble finding the....

*(She notices **AUGUST**.)*

...bathroom.

AUGUST. Holy shit.

LIZA. Hello, August.

AUGUST. Holy shit. It's you. Is it you?

LIZA. It's me.

AUGUST. Ho. Lee. SHIT. What the hell are you doing here?

LIZA. I was just telling your your / wife

DAPHNE. I will go make the omelet. Excuse me.

> (**DAPHNE** *exits.*)

LIZA. I was telling…she is STUNNING, by the way.

AUGUST. Thank you.

LIZA. And so YOUNG.

AUGUST. Thank you…Liza! Wha…

LIZA. I was in Rome, and Romania, and Prague, and Budapesht/

> (**AUGUST** *and* **LIZA** *begin kissing almost accidentally.*
> *Then they stop, embarrassed, surprised. Awkward.*)

> (**DAPHNE** *enters.*)

DAPHNE. You might like to know, they said on the radio. Your president has been elected. He is named Ronald Reagan.

> (**LIZA** *exits.* **AUGUST** *and* **DAPHNE** *move into similar*
> *positions they were before* **LIZA** *entered.*)

AUGUST. Who?

> (**DAPHNE** *does not answer.*)

> Daphne…

DAPHNE. The one who bites.

> (**LIZA** *enters.*)

LIZA. I had trouble finding the….

> (*She notices* **AUGUST**.)

> …*bathroom.*

AUGUST. Holy shit.

LIZA. Hello, August.

AUGUST. Holy shit . It's you. Is it you?

LIZA. It's me.

AUGUST. Ho. Lee. SHIT. What the hell are you doing here?

LIZA. I was just telling your your / wife

DAPHNE. I will go make the omelet. Excuse me.

(**DAPHNE** *exits.*)

LIZA. I was telling…she is STUNNING, by the way.

AUGUST. Thank you.

LIZA. And so YOUNG.

AUGUST. Thank you…Liza! Wha…

LIZA. I was in Rome, and Romania, and Prague, and Buda-pesht –

(*beat*)

Did you know that's how they pronounce it? With a 'sht'?

AUGUST. I'm, I'm literally

LIZA. PESSHHHT. I was doing some traveling, so…did you know Hungary has the highest, the highest um suicide rate of any other country? In the world?

AUGUST. You're a woman.

LIZA. Ha! I suppose I am.

AUGUST. You dropped all the baby fat.

LIZA. Ha! Well it was more like standard grade D American Chub…big Mac and a vanilla McShake every Mcfrickin' meal…

AUGUST. Are you hungry? Can I get you anything? Champagne? (*He dashes over to the champagne bucket.*)

LIZA. Strange we didn't see the irony of keeping our enemies in business…thanks…How is it that you look exactly the same?

AUGUST. I don't.

LIZA. You're swarthier, actually…

AUGUST. Swarthier? No.

LIZA. Not a little swarthier? Not even a little?

AUGUST. Knobbier, maybe. Less hair.

(*He hands her a glass of champagne, then realizes she still has her wine.*)

Oh, sorry, I didn't / even realize

LIZA. No, it's, hang on…

(**LIZA** *downs her glass quickly.* **AUGUST** *is amused.*)

AUGUST. You aren't a wine drinker.

LIZA. I'm no I don't suppose I mean a glass with dinner sometimes but.

AUGUST. *(mischievous)* Perfect. Are you as CLEVER as you ever were, Miss Liza?

LIZA. Clever-er, actually.

AUGUST. Then you shall learn. About such things. At this place. Are you as self-absorbed?

LIZA. You can't tell?

AUGUST. Then you will learn a lot, for fear of being made a fool.

LIZA. Ah. Well good.

AUGUST. Last question.

LIZA. Games, little August and his little / games

AUGUST. Are you still a raging lunatic?

LIZA. Well of course. It's in my nature.

(**AUGUST** *hands her a glass of champagne.*)

AUGUST. Then. Cheers.

(**DAPHNE** *enters with a large plate of eggs and three forks.* **AUGUST** *immediately begins wolfing it down.*)

DAPHNE. I make it like the French. With heavy cream. An old French lesbian showed me how. She said Americans don't eat eggs. She said Americans therefore are the dangerous people. She had chickens in her back.

AUGUST. Back*yard*. She didn't have chickens in her. Heh.

DAPHNE. Her eggs came to the kitchen still warm from the chickens' bodies. Once we found a beak in the egg. A little baby beak.

AUGUST. Daphne's family spent their summers at various chateaux in Normandy. LOADED...

(**DAPHNE** *offers a fork to* **LIZA.**)

LIZA. Thank you.

(**LIZA** *eats a forkful.*)

DAPHNE. My lesbian also told me it is customary to spit into the eggs of our enemies.

(**LIZA** *stops chewing.*)

Fortunately, I do not spit. Spitting is a dirt habit. For people who eat dirt. You agree?

AUGUST. Talking about spitting while one is eating is also a dirt habit, *mikri-kota-mou.*

DAPHNE. Only from those with the dirt-mouth. You are not eating, Liza.

LIZA. I'd like to be drunk first, thanks. Great eggs.

DAPHNE. Thank you. You might like to know, they said on the radio. Your president has been elected. He is named Ronald Reagan.

(*Slight beat, slight smile.*)

The actor.

(**LIZA** *and* **AUGUST** *look at each other.* **AUGUST** *drinks.*)

LIZA. I didn't realize you folks got American news over here.

DAPHNE. We receive the large news, the head – headlines, of course. We once received American newspapers to the house. But then I stopped allowing them. You know that vine in his neck, the big vine? When he would read the American news his vine would pop.

LIZA. Vein, I think. Right?

DAPHNE. He has a grape vine in his neck. Tell her, *Avgusto.*

AUGUST. I have a grape vine in my neck, Liza. It used to be a vein. But now when I bleed. My blood is wine. Delicious eggs, my filthy chicken. You know, tonight? We should have a feast. For Liza.

DAPHNE. Of course we should.

LIZA. Oh, no…

AUGUST. What do you eat?

LIZA. Don't go to any. I wasn't even planning on / staying

AUGUST. There are no other guest houses for miles.

LIZA. I eat everything.

AUGUST. A feast then. For the last day of harvest AND for a long lost friend. More champagne?

LIZA. No thank you. All right.

(He pours.)

DAPHNE. Liza! You are the first old friend of my husband's which whom I have met. I would very much like to hear a story from his youth.

LIZA. A story? Like what kind of…

DAPHNE. A badly behaved story. I'm sure he has many.

LIZA. Um…I met him senior year of high school, so…he was a, oh god a WRETCHED student. I mean he was a genius, but. But he liked to do, heh. Bad things. To teachers. Like have AFFAIRS with them.

AUGUST. Ha! I forgot about that!

LIZA. Oh please, how could you / have POSSIBLY

DAPHNE. Affairs. Love affairs.

AUGUST. Man oh / man…

DAPHNE. I am not shocked.

AUGUST. Just the one, Liza is hyperbolizing/

LIZA. One was / PLENNY

DAPHNE. I don't know that word, / Hyper…

LIZA. She was so OLD!

AUGUST. No she was / not.

LIZA. She was what, fifty, / fifty-five?

AUGUST. THIRTY-five. Ish.

DAPHNE. You were how / old?

AUGUST. I don't / recall

LIZA. Seventeen. He got EXPELLED. For BONING his chemistry teacher! She was, is, is this an appropriate / story

AUGUST.	DAPHNE.
It's fine.	Go on.

LIZA. Well he was planning on dropping out anyway. Was on this angsty kick against formal education.

AUGUST. Heh/

LIZA. Wanted to eat garbage and write leftist propaganda. They called him "Mega-Marx!"

AUGUST. You're leaving out the best part of the story!

LIZA. Oh! So this teacher wasn't just ANY teacher...she was BLACK. A BLACK teacher in a white public school system. In suburban New Jersey. In 1963. You can just imagine the uproar from the – do, do you know anything about the American Civil Rights movement?

DAPHNE. Yes.

LIZA. Well anyway. She got very fired AND very publicly ostracized...And a week later, he showed up to the board of ed meeting with about twenty angry teenagers.

All in blackface.

(**AUGUST** and **LIZA** laugh.)

DAPHNE. Ha. That is an amusing. I also know a story. It is one involving you.

LIZA. Really? What?

DAPHNE. I'm sure if you thought hard you would think it up.

LIZA. I am thinking hard...

AUGUST. Miss Liza, what is the one story my wife would have to know?

LIZA. I really can't imagine...

(**AUGUST** stands and turns his body to the side, and pulls down his pants. A puffy, bite-shaped scar is dug into his hip.)

DAPHNE. You and he were living out of your small car at the San Francisco Bay. You had no more food. You had not washed yourselves in two weeks besides your feet in the water. You had sex four times a day and were on pot much of the time. You were lying with your stringy head in his lap with your eyes closed. You were talking about molecules moving in your fingers and your feet. You were talking about how your skin was not solid, how the vinyl seat was not solid. You said everything was vibrating in nature at all times, and you said it scared you so much, and you said the only time you felt still was when his voice was in your ears, low and serious. And then you felt a wet drop on your closed lids, and you opened them and he was crying into your eyes. And he said you are so beautiful Liza, you are so beautiful you could crack the sky open. And you said August you are like the universe, you are so big you fill me you fill my ears and you fill me. He brought his head down to yours and unrolled his tongue into your mouth. And his fingers wound around your hair. And you grabbed his hip with your hand and you said the word NEED, and you wrapped your thick leg around his skinny leg and said the word NEED, and then you sank your teeth into his hip and bit so hard you came back with part of him in your mouth. And then you made love. And you fell asleep. And when you woke up you had a red smear on your face where you fell asleep in his blood. But he was gone.

That was the last time you saw him.

LIZA. Huh. I don't remember that.

AUGUST. You do, Liza.

LIZA. I don't, really. Biting. I'd remember a thing like that. But I do have the urge quite often. To bite people. I just don't think I'd follow it through.

AUGUST. Of course you would. You want to bite my wife right now. Admit it.

LIZA. Ha! Sure! I'll bite her face off!

AUGUST. I think you just might.

LIZA. What? Shut up.

DAPHNE. She will. She is about to.

LIZA. Bite your face? No, honey. I will not bite your face.

AUGUST. Do it. Go on. Bite her.

DAPHNE. August –

(Long beat. **LIZA** *looks as though she might bite*
DAPHNE's *face. She does. Chaos. Then…)*

DAPHNE. Ha. That is an amusing. I also know a story. It is
one involving you.

LIZA. Really? What?

DAPHNE. I'm sure if you thought hard you would think it
up.

LIZA. I am thinking hard…

AUGUST. Miss Liza, what is the one story my wife would
have to know?

LIZA. I really can't imagine…

*(**AUGUST** stands and digs into his pocket, and takes out
a package of Wint-O-green Lifesavers.)*

Oh NO!!

*(He pops three in his mouth and begins to chew, smiling
hugely.* **LIZA** *begins cracking up.)*

DAPHNE. He is obsessed. Impossible to get over here, I
have / them shipped.

LIZA. You told her!

AUGUST.	**DAPHNE.**
No choice, I'm /afraid	He tells me everything

LIZA. Roll after roll, / the whole trip…

AUGUST. Ha ha!

LIZA. Getting high in our car every night, reading passages
from Reagan's autobiography –

AUGUST. It had a great title, didn't it, a line in a movie
where he played an amputee…um…"Where's the Rest
of Me. The Ronald Reagan Story."

DAPHNE. What/ ah…

LIZA. That's it! And THEN, we'd turn off our flashlights
and you'd haul out the Wint-o-greens…

AUGUST. Fireworks!! Every time!! God that was…it was
epic. Wasn't it?

LIZA. It was. And you had like a theory, a real scientific THING / for the whole

AUGUST. Not theory. Fact. All hard sugar-based candies emit some degree of light when you bite them. It's called um triboluminescence.

DAPHNE. I don't know that / word

AUGUST. The emission of light resulting from something being smashed or, or / torn.

LIZA. You ass. It's MAGIC. A little electrical storm in your mouth.

AUGUST. But well YES. That's exactly what it is.

DAPHNE. Don't think me rude for saying this but I feel as though you should not be calling my husband a donkey. Thank you. Pardon me...

(**DAPHNE** *begins cleaning up the dishes.*)

"Boning." This means to make love.

AUGUST. ...yes.

DAPHNE. I was not certain.

(**DAPHNE** *exits. A beat.*)

AUGUST. Well.

LIZA. Well.

(*small beat*)

AUGUST. Fucking Reagan –

LIZA. I KNOW! I mean he was way ahead in the polls this week, but I thought maybe, just maybe.... I mean not really but.

AUGUST. Were you in on any of that?

LIZA. I tried, man. We were going door to door right up until I got on the plane.

AUGUST. Not for Carter?

LIZA. God no. Voter registration. I work for the ACLU. We focus on former convicts, the disenfranchised, et cetera.

AUGUST. *(impressed)* Pounding the pavement for / the people's rights...

LIZA. Well mostly I'm behind a desk in a tiny grey office drinking bad coffee and working for pennies. But yeah.

AUGUST. Where?

LIZA. Berkeley.

AUGUST. Still?

LIZA. Jealous?

AUGUST. I am. We had quite a little thing going, didn't we. Sweating into our Keds outside / the Safeway...

LIZA. The Safeway, yeah

AUGUST. ...looting AV equipment from the student union...

LIZA. We kept at it after you left. Got pretty close. We were only about two hundred thousand signatures away from qualifying for the ballot to kick Reagan out of the governor's office...

AUGUST. Wow. That's –

LIZA. Fat lotta good it did.

AUGUST. Still. You tried.

(small beat)

LIZA. We fell apart two weeks later. We needed you man. Everyone wanted to know where you had gone. I told them Canada. Said you'd be back when the draft was over. I went looking, once...Mendecino, Humbolt, Crescent City even...

Not even a postcard.

(beat)

You gonna tell me what happened?

AUGUST. *(with difficulty)* Yeah, okay.

I was making this speech one day – it was a Thursday, that's when I had the morning shift at the Copymat – so I had this stack of stolen flyers, and I was screaming about how everyone should hurl their bodies onto the gears of the machine, right...but for some reason I started getting panicky...then I was floating above myself, looking down at the throngs of kids...and suddenly it was like *I was* the machine...So I just, I fucking lost it. Grabbed the stack of flyers and chucked them at the crowd. Left town the next day.

(beat)

LIZA. I'm sorry.

AUGUST. You couldn't have done anything. Some people were meant for greatness. I'm not one of them.

(A long beat. **AUGUST** *drinks.)*

LIZA. *(trying)* But...you're doing something here, right? Something big? With your vineyard? Your wife said –

AUGUST. I'm trying...

LIZA. She said you're revolutionizing the wine industry.

AUGUST. I'm *trying*. I planted a rare varietal.

LIZA. What's that?

AUGUST. A derivation of a common regional grape called *mavrodaphne*. Traditionally it is a sweet communion wine, but I vinified a DRY *mavrodaphne*. This country has no wine trade, so if it takes off...well the economy here could use it...and we'd have a cheap decent bottle for the locals, so...
That's something. Right?

LIZA. Hell yeah. That's fucking amazing!

AUGUST. You think?

LIZA. Yeah! It's great, August. You – you have this – eating the world with your eyes kind of thing...

*(***DAPHNE*** *emerges. She is dressed differently, more elegantly, but still appropriate, possibly in a flowered dress. She is now wearing make-up. She carries freshly cut flowers. They are odd and wild and beautiful.)*

DAPHNE. I feel better now. It is a superb weather today. This year's harvest will be extraordinary, with this orange sun and thickly spiced air...

AUGUST. Did Daphne show you the label? Show her, Kota...

(**DAPHNE** *retrieves a print from her work area. She shows*
LIZA.)

DAPHNE. It is not done...you see I need to fill in the details
on the leaves. Also the wood grain on the barrels.

(**LIZA** *examines the print.*)

LIZA. I like it.

DAPHNE. *Avgusto* does not.

AUGUST. I love it. It's just, it's a little. Stately, but.

DAPHNE. He wants it to have more whimsy and wickedness.

AUGUST. It's beautiful.

LIZA. Where's the, the thingie. The title.

DAPHNE. The name is secret. He will not tell even me. I
think he does not have one.

AUGUST. Oh I have a name. It is top secret. I want to taste it
first before I make it official.

LIZA. You haven't tasted it?

AUGUST. I'm superstitious. Two more days, Liza. I feel like
a little kid. Will you still be here?

LIZA. Do you want me to be?

AUGUST. Of course, yes, I would very much like you to stay
for it.

LIZA. Would you.

AUGUST. I...ha.

LIZA. Could you tell me where the bathroom is?

AUGUST. Through the kitchen and down the uh, the stairs.

LIZA. Thank you. Whoo. I'm a little. Tipsy, actually I might
like to nap. I didn't sleep much on the. Boat, a baby
kept crying...

DAPHNE. Of course. I will come down with a glass of water
for you shortly.

LIZA. No need...

DAPHNE. Very well. Shall you have a legend when you come
back?

LIZA. That's /okay

DAPHNE. Has she earned a legend, *Avgusto?*

AUGUST. *(playful)* Indeed. She's earned *two.*

LIZA. Swell. See you in a while.

AUGUST. Sleep well...

> *(She exits.* **AUGUST** *and* **DAPHNE** *are tense around each other a moment.)*

DAPHNE. *Thelo na sou 'po, then nomizo oti prepi na ine 'tho / avrio yia toh –* *(Translation:* "I have to say, I don't think she should be here tomorrow for the –")

AUGUST. English, Kota, I'm too tired to translate...

DAPHNE. Uurrg. I am weary of English. It is such a pointy language. Many corners and very little curves. I feel when I speak it I am walking around a small room with large pieces of sharp furniture.

AUGUST. It's good practice. You're out of practice.

DAPHNE. I also feel this way around your friend...

> *(a beat)*

You told me she was dead.

AUGUST. I said she was *probably* dead.

DAPHNE. Why do you imagine she's here?

AUGUST. She's traveling...

DAPHNE. It is not usual.

AUGUST. She saw a posting. We're in that book, they all have the same guidebook.

DAPHNE. Will she be paying?

AUGUST. She's our guest, Daphne.

DAPHNE. She was not invited. We need the money. I cannot bear to go to my father again. Not after last time.

AUGUST. I'll ask her to leave. Would you like that?

DAPHNE. I do not think she should be here for the tasting.

AUGUST. Why not?

DAPHNE. It is an intimate moment. You do not know what to expect. It could be a triumph but also it could be a disappointment –

> *(**LIZA** reappears.)*

LIZA. Sorry. There's a girl in the bed.

DAPHNE. That is Boy. He is passed out. Just move him gently to one side.

LIZA. Oh. Okay.

(**LIZA** *disappears. A beat.*)

AUGUST. I'll tell her we need the rooms. Or that you aren't up to entertaining. I'll think of something.

(**DAPHNE** *begins scraping into her block in agitation.*)

She was never good around other women. Didn't have many girlfriends. Hid in corners, that sort of. People thought she was mental. Got into fights a lot, this thing she'd do…I thought it was funny at the time. She'd bring a, a pair of scissors to class and snip the hair of whoever sat in front of her.

DAPHNE. Oh. I like that.

AUGUST. You would have been the girl whose hair was snipped.

DAPHNE. Do not be ridiculous. I commanded respect at that age. I had many friends, even the ugly girls. They threw a party of me at fifteen. It was a surprise. I remember I had stolen a dress that day. Did I tell you about this?

AUGUST. No.

DAPHNE. I stole a designer dress from the department store. I could have bought it myself. I had the money…It was a very pretty dress. It had sparkle, you know? Those bits that catch the light. Not diamonds, the other word. But I didn't want it badly enough to pay. And it was my birthday. I thought if I got caught I would tell the men it is my birthday, and they would let me take it anyway. But I did not get caught. In the room where you try things on, I put on the dress, then I put on my longer dress over it, and then I walked home. And my heart was so light. And I arrived home and my house was full of my friends, all smiling and eating little foods on plates. And there was a pile of *cadeaux* in the corner, eh, gifts. And I took off my long dress and beneath I was sparkling, and everyone shouted "ahhh!" and applauded. As if I could have known I had a party waiting for me. It was luck! I've always been lucky like that.

AUGUST. I bet you were beautiful.

DAPHNE. I could sparkle for you now, if you like. I will become a holiday. I will decorate myself with twinkle lights and sing a song about a man who buries his heart in the dirt and later eats the dirt to remember how the heart tasted.

I will behave myself around your *amour perdu...*

AUGUST. You're fine.

(**DAPHNE** *begins to Greek dance a little, her arms out.* **AUGUST** *watches her.*)

Look. Can you see them? My twinkle lights...

(**DAPHNE** *turns on the radio from before. She dances for him. He claps along half-heartedly. She pulls* **AUGUST** *from his seat.*)

AUGUST. Too tired, *kota...*

DAPHNE. This will enervise you...

(**AUGUST** *begins dancing.* **AUGUST**'s *steps are clumsy.*)

Your Greek dancing is appalling.

AUGUST. I'm not greek.

DAPHNE. Can you not get your back any straighter?

AUGUST. It doesn't go any straighter.

DAPHNE. Of course it does.

(**AUGUST** *begins dancing absurdly.*)

AUGUST. *Opa!!*

DAPHNE. Don't say that. You sound like an American.

AUGUST. *Opa!! Opa!! Ella! Yia-sou!*

(**AUGUST** *stops dancing.*)

DAPHNE. An insult to my people...

AUGUST. I'll take lessons...

DAPHNE. You are beyond correction...

AUGUST. Find me a teacher.

(small beat)

DAPHNE. *(melancholy, distant)* There are no men in the village who would teach a husband of mine.

AUGUST. Don't think about that right now...

*(**AUGUST** draws **DAPHNE** into her. They slow-dance.)*

DAPHNE. My father had a friend, and old man...at every wedding he would dance for hours. His jumps were so high. Balloon, they used to call him. You could not stop him. Not even to feed him. He is dead now...

AUGUST. Did he dance himself to death?

DAPHNE. Yes.

*(**AUGUST** stops dancing.)*

AUGUST. Are you trying to kill me, *kota?*

DAPHNE. Yes.

AUGUST. But you aren't a dangerous woman. You are a brown bean.

DAPHNE. Would you like me to be dangerous? I could be.

AUGUST. No...

DAPHNE. I have a little danger in me. A very little.

AUGUST. I know where your danger is.

(He touches her belly, then below.)

DAPHNE. Yes...

AUGUST. Filthy...filthy...

DAPHNE. *Ne...*

(They begin kissing passionately.)

(Lights down. They continue kissing as...)

(A radio broadcast is heard. Music, scratchy, news from America, spoken with an English accent.)

ANNOUNCER. *(V.O.)* This is the BBC. Now your news from America.

The former Hollywood actor and Republican governor of California Ronald Reagan is to be the next president of the United States. He has defeated Democrat Jimmy Carter in the US presidential elections by a landslide. The last speech of Mr. Reagan's campaign was followed by a dazzling firework display, after which he returned to his home in Pacific Palisades to spend polling day resting.

During the next 30 years, certain sectors of the global economy will experience unprecedented levels of growth, due to Reagan's deregulatory approach. Many industries, including winemaking, will enjoy an unexpected boom. People will spend beyond their means, buy homes they cannot afford, borrow money from corrupt sources. But eventually, the bubble shall pop. This will of course result in a world-wide financial crisis. One of the casualties of this disaster will be Greece.

In other news...things often burst. They burst.

(Lights up on the porch. It is eight hours later. The remains of a huge feast lies out on the table. Two empty bottles of wine and one half-empty bottle are on the table.)

*(**LIZA** sits at the table alone. She surveys the carnage of the meal and chomps Wint-o-green after Wint-o-green. She is distant, troubled.)*

*(**BOY**, a teen-aged girl dressed as a **BOY** in jeans and a cap, sneaks onto the porch. She is covered in soil and her fingertips are stained red. She walks sloppily and slouchy, all elbows and hips.)*

*(**BOY** loads up a plate of food for herself. She then moves to the corner and eats in silence, taking occasional swigs from a bottle of half-drunk wine.)*

(a beat)

LIZA. Do you live here?

    (**BOY** *doesn't answer.*)

    Before…earlier, I mean, in the…

    (**BOY** *doesn't answer.*)

    Do you speak? At all?

    (**BOY** *guzzles her wine.*)

    Where are your parents?

    (**DAPHNE** *enters.*)

DAPHNE. *(to* **LIZA***)* Kali spera. Have you eaten enough? *(Translation:* "Good evening.")

LIZA. Um yeah. Enough for a week…

DAPHNE. I am sorry you did not come on our walk with us. The sun setting onto the hill is *poli orea*. Very beautiful.

LIZA. Sunset, christ…we were eating three hours straight…

DAPHNE. Yes. We do this. Lengthy eating. It is fortunate I enjoy to cook. It calms me. Did you know in Greece we have eighty-six ways to say "stop feeding me?"

LIZA. Why does that not surprise me.

DAPHNE. I do not understand the question.

LIZA. No, it. I meant. That it doesn't surprise me.

DAPHNE. Are you not easily surprised?

LIZA. Actually. Everything surprises me.

DAPHNE. Do I surprise you?

LIZA. In what way?

DAPHNE. When you first appeared you said I was beautiful, and then you said you were not prepared. This reveals you had an expectation. "The wife of *Avgusto* will be unattractive."

    (**LIZA** *laughs.*)

    You laugh because it rings of truth.

LIZA. Well I suppose I "expected" him to be with a woman who was alive when Kennedy was shot.

DAPHNE. I was alive. I was seven.

LIZA. Right.

DAPHNE. Does the age difference affect you?

LIZA. I was kidding / around

DAPHNE. American women are threatened by age. Why is this?

LIZA. Well, I don't know too many American women, so.

DAPHNE. No, I suppose you are uncommon. *Avgusto* would not care for a common woman.

(**DAPHNE** *smiles hugely.*)

You see how I compliment you and turn it back around to me? That is a cultural thing.

French, I mean. I identify often with the French. Greek women tend to be more. There is an English word that means "under the service of men"...

LIZA. And you aren't?

DAPHNE. Of course I am. But it is different when the man is equally under the service of the woman. Yes?

LIZA. Ah.

(*A beat.* **LIZA** *peers around.*)

So is, is he...

DAPHNE. He will be up shortly. He said he has getting something special. *Is.*

LIZA. Not dessert I hope.

DAPHNE. He did not say.

(*an awkward silence*)

Tell me about where you live.

LIZA. I'd rather not.

DAPHNE. Why?

LIZA. I'm in transition.

DAPHNE. Surely you have a place to hang your clothing.

LIZA. I don't own a tremendous amount of clothing.

DAPHNE. You are being coy.

LIZA. No. I had, I DID have an apartment. In a building.

DAPHNE. A tall building? A "sky..." a sky/

LIZA. Not really. It, um. Six stories. Old carpet. The elevator is always broken. A radiator, um, you know don't take this the wrong way? I am not. Good at this. Aimless chatter. I kind of hate it.

DAPHNE. You are doing beautifully.

LIZA. I kind of really hate it.

(a beat)

And now, you're. Um LOOKING at me, so, and I, I already talked about the food, and the view, the sunset, and I don't really want to talk about August, so.

Is there more wine?

(DAPHNE *walks over to* **BOY** *and pries the bottle from her hands, pouring* **LIZA** *a glass. She returns the bottle to* **BOY**, *who continues to guzzle it.)*

DAPHNE. Liza, I feel I must be frank to you. I do not trust you. BUT, it is one of the reasons I feel so compelled by you.

LIZA. Oh.

DAPHNE. And you both speak very fast around one another, which also makes me feel strange.

LIZA. It's chilly, isn't it?

DAPHNE. We are without friends here and I feel grateful for your company and therefore I feel generous toward you. I wonder if you would like Boy to help you with anything.

LIZA. No. Should she be/ drink

DAPHNE. He is fine.

LIZA. Can she, okay, *he* speak English?

DAPHNE. Only how are you and have a nice day.

LIZA. He, actually she. Before, when I was sleeping.

DAPHNE. Yes. He likes to massage sometimes. Do not let it offend you. I wonder if it felt nice, though.

LIZA. Um.

DAPHNE. It is meant to relax you.

LIZA. Oh.

DAPHNE. I will mention to him not to do it again. But let us continue to talk frankly. I would like you to tell me something. With being frank.

LIZA. With being frank. Okay.

DAPHNE. Why are you here.

LIZA. That's a great question, Daphne. I'll answer it. Sure, no problem. I'll answer your question. I have no problem answering that question.

(*They stare each other down for several moments. It should be so long it looks as though both actors have forgotten their lines. REALLY long. No shorter than twenty seconds.*)

DAPHNE. But let us continue to talk frankly. I would like you to tell me something. With being frank.

LIZA. With being frank. Okay.

DAPHNE. Why are you here.

LIZA. I have something belonging to August that I need to return.

(*A long beat. **DAPHNE** smiles.*)

DAPHNE. I love the American sense of humor.

(***LIZA** stares blankly at her.*)

(*Some time passes where neither women say a word.*)

Perhaps you shall tell me later.

(***AUGUST** is hooting offstage. He enters holding something in a bag very preciously..*)

LIZA. Finally! What took you so long?

AUGUST. I was having a moment of. Of rapture, one could say?

(*He places the bag gently onto the table.*)

You missed a freakin' PHENOMENAL sunset, / Liza-Maria.

LIZA. I heard…

AUGUST. Haven't seen a sunset like that since our first harvest, remember Daphne?

DAPHNE. I / do

AUGUST. The sky all bloody and diabolical…Christ I can't *wait* to taste it. Thirty-seven hours…

(**AUGUST** *notices* **BOY** *in the corner. She has passed out. He kicks at his feet.*)

(playful) Hey! *Ine mono yia tous megaloos!* Adults only! *Fee'yeh apo 'do.* (*Translation:* "This is FOR ADULTS ONLY! Adults only. Get out of here.")

BOY. *Ande gameesoo, ye-ro!* (*Translation:* "Fuck you old man!")

AUGUST. *(amused)* Ho! Did you hear that?

DAPHNE. The mouth on him!

AUGUST. *Prosekse, ee tha reekso krio nero sta moo'tra soo san kee'mase…* (*Translation:* "Watch out, or I'll dump a cup of cold water on your head while you sleep…")

BOY. *Eho panta ina matee anee'hto. Kai ime pyo gree'goros apo 'sena.* (*Translation:* "I sleep with one eye open. And I'm faster than you.")

(*They scuffle playfully.*)

DAPHNE. *(laughing)* Be careful, you'll hurt him!

LIZA. Why do you keep doing that? Calling her a him?

AUGUST. Just a game….

(**AUGUST** *hands* **BOY** *the open bottle of wine.*)

Go on!

(**BOY** *exits.*)

Now. We have some veeeery important business to attend to. Ahem. Close your eyes, Liza.

DAPHNE. *Thavmastiko! Ti Hara!* This will be fun… (*Translation:* "Wonderful! How fun!")

LIZA. W-what's / going on –

AUGUST. Close 'em!

LIZA. Jeez, okay!

(**LIZA** *closes her eyes. This is the ultimate game.*)

AUGUST. *(fun, painting a picture)* Ready?
> Legend one.
>
> It is May 1906. We are in the southwest of France, the *Medoc* region. We are at a famous Chateau, which makes a very famous Bordeaux. It is a warm and rainy spring. Can you feel it?

LIZA. Definitely…

DAPHNE. *(to LIZA)* He loves telling this…

> *(Throughout, it is AUGUST telling the story and DAPHNE making playful sound-effects, helping to tell it. It is their story…until it becomes LIZA's.)*

AUGUST. We are kneeling in a small, experimental patch of vines. We are a young man and a young woman. We are slowly taking off one another's clothes.

LIZA. Oooh! Which one am I?

AUGUST. Either, both. We do this every day, explore each other when we should be tending the vines. We cannot help ourselves.

LIZA. Mmmmm.

AUGUST. Our vineyard manager does not see us. He is more concerned with the main plots. But he is in love with one of us. Fiercely. There is history here.

LIZA. Racy!

AUGUST. Indeed! The spring months ripen into summer, and the world goes hot and dry. But we do not notice. And when our vines are attacked by deadly moths, we do not notice.
> But he does. He comes down the hill early one morning, and he sees…one hand in the other's hair, one hand in the other's mouth. He tears us apart and slaps one of us in the face, the one whom he loves. The unslapped one flees the vineyard in a hot wash of shame.

LIZA. Oh…

AUGUST. The slapped one remains, and must do the work of two, and quickly, as the moth infestation is spreading.

Then. Press press press, into the wire grid, press press fingers wrinkled and stained purple, press press press press press press press press press press press press.... The million minor cuts are the last things to touch these grapes. The grapes, conversely, are the last things to touch these young hands in this field during this hot dry September in 1906...for late one evening, on the last day of harvest, the blade of the vine scissors will slice...Two. Young. Wrists.

LIZA. Jesus....

(**AUGUST** *pauses long.*)

DAPHNE. Only twenty bottles were produced from this slim crop. And –

(*He shuts* **DAPHNE** *down with a curt gesture and a sound.*)

AUGUST. Twenty bottles were produced. And they are legendary.

(**DAPHNE** *moves elsewhere to pout while he continues without her.*)

(**AUGUST** *touches the wine holder.*)

AUGUST. *(cont.)* Six of the bottles were lost in an estate fire in 1940. Three bottles were auctioned off to a Swiss heir in the 30's. A German wine collector boasts of owning five bottles himself. Three bottles are unaccounted for. Two bottles have been sampled at vertical tastings, one in '64 and one in '73, and both times the wines were described as "astonishing."

(**AUGUST** *unsheathes the old, dusty bottle. It has a crusted yellowing etched label. He holds it sideways, presenting it.*)

And one of the bottles, Liza, is here.

(**LIZA** *opens her eyes...and sees the bottle...and gasps a little.*)

We spent every penny we had on this. It was worth twice that.

(a long beat)

LIZA. You're going to open it now, aren't you.

(AUGUST takes a moment to decide. Then, he places the bottle upright.)

AUGUST. Blame the sunset. Blame the harvest.

LIZA. *(electrified)* Oh my God...

AUGUST. I always knew I'd *feel* when the right moment came along. And I swore to myself I would not let it pass. People do that, they. Second guess themselves...

LIZA. But you never do, August.

AUGUST. No, Bitchadeeto. I do not.

LIZA. Oh my gosh oh my gosh...

(AUGUST removes a bottle opener from his pocket. **DAPHNE** *is stone.)*

AUGUST. This probably won't work, the uh. Cork might be a little decrepit...

(AUGUST places three huge-globed wine glasses on the table. He then retrieves a very long-necked glass decanter. He gestures to the candle.)

AUGUST. *(cont.)* Light that.

(LIZA lights the candle.)

(AUGUST lines it up next to the neck of the bottle, peering at it through the glass. Then he wipes down the bottle with a cloth and very carefully removes the cork.)

...got most of it...

(He smells the cork, then wipes down the neck of the bottle again.)

LIZA. So exciting...my heart is pounding...

(He places the decanter beneath the mouth of the bottle. He places both elbows on the table and very slowly, he begins to pour.)

(The wine begins to flow steadily, slowly, along the side of the decanter.)

(He watches the neck closely, lit by the candle.)

AUGUST. ...no one make me laugh...

LIZA. What's the candle for?

AUGUST. To see the sediment at the shoulder...shhhh.

(The decanter fills.)

Daphne. Can you believe we're doing this?

DAPHNE. No.

AUGUST. ...look at that color...

LIZA. Someone should take a picture...

*(**DAPHNE** retrieves her camera. She aims the lens at* **LIZA.***)*

Not, not me...him.

*(**DAPHNE** continues to focus on **LIZA.**)*

HIM...

DAPHNE. I want to remember this moment. Every detail.

*(**LIZA** hides her face with her hair. **DAPHNE** takes the picture.)*

AUGUST. ...almost there...

*(**DAPHNE** turns the camera on **AUGUST**. He smiles goofily. She snaps a picture.)*

(The decanter is full.)

*(**AUGUST** carefully pours wine into the three glasses.* **DAPHNE** *takes another picture.)*

Okay. Ladies, retrieve your glasses. We are about to drink history.

*(**LIZA** retrieves her glass.)*

*(**DAPHNE** very calmly places her camera on the table next to the wine.)*

DAPHNE. Goodnight, *Avgusto.*

(She exits.)

*(**AUGUST** and **LIZA** are silent a moment, holding their glasses.)*

LIZA. Um, okay what...?

AUGUST. Oh.

LIZA. ...What...

AUGUST. Oh. Oh.

(*He sinks to the ground in misery.*)

LIZA. August...

AUGUST. I totally, I completely...she's pregnant.

(**LIZA** *begins to hyperventilate. She crushes the glass in her hand. Her fist explodes in wine.* **AUGUST** *does not notice.* **LIZA** *retrieves another glass.*)

AUGUST. She's pregnant.

LIZA. I really like this wi –

(**LIZA** *crushes another glass.* **LIZA** *retrieves another.*)

AUGUST. She's pregnant.

LIZA. But. She saw you take three glasses out, she didn't say anything...

AUGUST. I should have...You know? *Immediately.*

LIZA. Why didn't she SAY some / thing?

AUGUST. It's not her style. DAMN IT!

LIZA. Style? That's ridicul / ous

AUGUST. Not everyone expresses everything.

LIZA. Maybe it's an age thing...

AUGUST. No. It's a *her* thing.

LIZA. Well.

(*a long beat*)

(*mean*) You're uh...you're gonna make a great fuckin' dad.

(*another long beat*)

Aren't you, you're not gonna go down there / and try to

AUGUST. No, no. She's otherwise occupied by now I'm sure.

LIZA. Oh. What does that / mean

AUGUST. Nothing.

(a beat)

LIZA. So. Um what I'm holding in my hand? Is basically your life's savings.

AUGUST. Pretty much.

LIZA. Wonder if Karl Marx ever spent his life's savings on a bottle of wine...

AUGUST. Probably not.

(a beat)

LIZA. You aren't going to let it go to waste, are you?

*(**AUGUST** holds the glass up to the moon.)*

AUGUST. Hold your glass up to the moon.

*(**LIZA** holds the glass up by the globe.)*

By the stem.

*(**LIZA** switches her grip.)*

See how clear the moon is through the wine?

LIZA. Yeah.

AUGUST. That's a very very good sign.

LIZA. Of what?

AUGUST. That your mind is about to be blown.

LIZA. Okay.

AUGUST. Swirl it in your glass.

(She does. He does.)

Now tip your nose in. Inhale.

(She does. He does.)

Now take only a little...wash your entire mouth in it... feel it on every bump on your tongue...

(She does. He does.)

Oh...oh...

(His eyes remain shut, his mouth working aggressively. He is tasting the hell out of the wine, for a really long time.)

(After a while...)

AUGUST. Just....

LIZA. Right?

AUGUST. I know.

LIZA. This.

AUGUST. I couldn't have even...

LIZA. ...is a beverage...

(He opens his eyes. They kiss sensuously.)

(a beat)

AUGUST. Thank you.

LIZA. No problem.

(a beat)

AUGUST. You should...keep drinking, the uh. Because it's old, the longer it sits out and oxidizes the more its. Quality declines. ...

(AUGUST sips.)

LIZA. Night of a thousand legends.

AUGUST. Got any for me?

LIZA. One. But I might save it.

AUGUST. For a rainy day? It doesn't rain in Greece in the fall...

LIZA. It does in Berkeley. Maybe I'll bring you back with me.

AUGUST. You'd bring me back just to get rained on?

LIZA. Among other things...

AUGUST. Ho ho...

(AUGUST drinks.)

LIZA. *(quietly)* Kiss me. Kiss me. Kiss me. Kiss me. Kiss me.

AUGUST. You *do* know Karl Marx was an inveterate wine drinker...

(AUGUST, having not heard her, quickly kisses her head.)

LIZA. I didn't...

AUGUST. His family owned a vineyard. He used to make Engles ship bottles of Bordeaux to him in, in London…

(A small beat. LIZA drinks.)

(quietly) Touch me. Touch me. Touch me. Touch me.

(LIZA places a hand on AUGUST's thigh.)

LIZA. I have a. Small confession.

AUGUST. Should I be sober for this?

LIZA. It's small…I've never been to Budapest. PESHT.

AUGUST. What about Prague?

LIZA. Nope.

AUGUST. Romania, Italy…

LIZA. Nope, nope. Came straight here.

AUGUST. Well done, Polita. You had me fooled.

LIZA. I practiced on the boat over.

AUGUST. You are a wily woman.

LIZA. Thank you.

AUGUST. Not sure it was a compliment.

LIZA. I know.

(beat)

AUGUST. Your hand is on my thigh, Liza.

LIZA. I know.

AUGUST. Do you plan on keeping it there?

LIZA. Hard to say.

AUGUST. Because I can't think straight with it there.

LIZA. Well I can't seem to move it.

AUGUST. I see.

(LIZA moves her hand higher on AUGUST's thigh.)

LIZA. Move it yourself.

(AUGUST slowly lifts her hand from his thigh and places it to his lips, closing his eyes. AUGUST kisses LIZA's fingers as though he is drinking her flesh.)

(Then, AUGUST bites into LIZA's wrist, hard. She gasps a little in pain.)

LIZA. *(whisper)* …harder…

(A beat. AUGUST removes his mouth from LIZA's arm. A beat. He lifts his glass to his lips and takes a slow sip.)

(LIZA rubs her wrist.)

(A long beat. AUGUST does not look at LIZA.)

I can wait….

(LIZA stands and exits.)

(AUGUST remains onstage, drinking the remains of the bottle alone.)

(Lights down.)

End of Act One

ACT TWO

(In the near fading darkness, we hear quietly, intimately, seductively, in voiceover:)

AUGUST. *(V.O.)* Legend two. Zeus killed Semele accidentally with a lightening bolt, whoops, while she was carrying his child...the baby Dionysus. Zeus rescued the fetus from her belly and sliced open his own thigh, where he placed the child until it was ready to be born. Then he delivered the infant to the nymphs for them to raise. So Baby Dionysus...well, he had a touch of the kookies. Maybe because of the thigh. He had followers, a ragtag pack of satyrs, sileni, maenads, and nymphs, who danced and drank all the time, and were fierce and rowdy, and had bloody sacrificial rites to try to merge their identities with nature.

Maybe they weren't eating enough dirt.

(Meanwhile, the lights slowly rise on LIZA in her pajamas. She makes her way to the table...or perhaps she is already there...After a long beat...)

LIZA. Legend three.

(a beat)

Legend three.

(a beat)

The third legend.... is...

(Lights on full. It is morning on the vineyard. LIZA is once again alone. She is alone for quite a while. Troubled.)

(Finally, DAPHNE enters with a bright expression on her face.)

DAPHNE. *Kali Mera, Americaneetha.* Would you like some Greek coffee? We also have Folders. The crystals.

LIZA. Fol-GERS.

DAPHNE. Fol-GERS, excuse me. You look very bad. As though you were awake all the night. So I will give you the Greek coffee. Thick and sweet and strong. Boy? *Agory?*

(**BOY** *enters.*)

Yia-sou, agapi-mou...Ehh, ftyakse tin Americaneetha ligo cafédaki, glyko, parakalo? Ke doseh-tin, ehh, yaourti me meli, ke...ligo psomi, ke...fruito. Meela, ne? (Translation: "Hello love. Ehh, bring the American a little sweet coffee please? And bring her, ehh, yogurt with honey, and...a little bread, and...fruit. Apples, yes?")

BOY. *Endaksi. (Translation:* "Okay.")

DAPHNE. *Efharisto. (Translation:* "Thank you.")

(**BOY** *exits. A beat.*)

Do you have any plans for the day?

LIZA. I don't know.

DAPHNE. The radio says there is a sale at an Italian shoe store at the Eurocenter today. It is not far from here, but I do not drive so we would need *Avgusto* to driving us. I do not have much affection for the Eurocenter, it is a bit coarse and smells like a swimming pool. But the stores are very good.

LIZA. I don't need shoes.

DAPHNE. Yes, but you may like to looking at them. Often I go and do not purchase anything, I just admire. It shall be dull here for you if we go...

(**LIZA** *looks around uncomfortably.*)

You are uncomfortable with me still! Is this because you want to make love with my husband? To be frank, I was hoping you would last night. I am puzzled to why this did not occur. But do it soon, so perhaps we may all be more relaxed for your visit.

LIZA. Sorry?

DAPHNE. I am a very flexible woman. Which is where you and I differ, I believe. Also, I do not like violence during love-making, and I am sure he misses this sometimes...

LIZA. Uh...that's, / that's really

DAPHNE. And I want to say this also: I will not continue to feed someone who insists on being my rival. I hope you understand.

LIZA. I do.

DAPHNE. Good.

(**AUGUST** *enters, looking slightly hung over.*)

Kali mera. Your friend and I were just discussing you. *(Translation:* "Good morning.")

AUGUST. What were you discussing?

DAPHNE. I was saying I wished you had made love to her last night.

AUGUST. That's very adorable of you.

DAPHNE. I was saying you yearn to have sexual violence.

AUGUST. We can do without this over breakfast, *ne kota?* *(Translation:* "yes chicken?")

DAPHNE. You are like a little sour boy. Does your head hurt from the *krassaki?* ("wine")

AUGUST. Yes.

DAPHNE. I hope you shared some with your friend.

AUGUST. I did.

(**BOY** *enters with a tray filled with yogurt, apples, coffee and bread.*)

DAPHNE. There. We have yogurt, honey, apples, coffee and fresh bread. The coffee is already sweetened.

(*to* **BOY**)

Ella, katse mazimas... (*Translation:* "Come here, sit down.")

BOY. *Ohi...then pinao...* (*Translation:* "No...I'm not hungry.")

(**BOY** *moves off to the side and sets up a table with a manual juice press.*)

AUGUST. Not hungry? That's a first…

DAPHNE. Is he sick? *Agory, ise arostos? (Translation:* "Boy, are you sick?")

(**BOY** *shakes her head retrieves a basket of fresh oranges to be juiced. She has her eye on* **DAPHNE**. **DAPHNE** *ignores her.*)

(*All begin eating quietly, awkwardly.*)

(*after a beat*)

If you are not too sleepy *Avgusto* I would like a ride to the Eurocenter today. There is a sale on shoes.

AUGUST. We have no money, *kota.*

DAPHNE. I am just going to look. And your friend would like to come as well.

(**AUGUST** *looks at* **LIZA**.)

AUGUST. You're going shopping together?

DAPHNE. And you do not have to shop with us. They are showing a movie in the cinema down the road. The Raging Bull. It is around a boxing man.

(**AUGUST** *chuckles.*)

Something is humorous?

AUGUST. Ah, no, well yes, the image of Liza buying shoes, actually.

DAPHNE. She wears shoes, does she not?

(*to* **LIZA**)

You wear shoes, do you not?

LIZA. I wear shoes.

AUGUST. She doesn't want to do that, Liza, do you want to do that? Go shopping? At the Eurocenter?

LIZA. I do.

DAPHNE. And you have not seen a film in a while, so go to that and we will shop. And we will get a gift for Boy also, for working so hard this year.

(**DAPHNE** *smiles at* **BOY**. **BOY** *walks over to the radio and changes the station. Blondie's "Call Me" begins to play.**)

He despises the folk music. It depresses him.

(**BOY** *turns the volume up and returns to her oranges, singing softly. She squeezes them with a manual press and dances somewhat sexily while doing so, feigning nonchalance...but clearly this is a performance for* **DAPHNE**.)

(**BOY** *has no idea what she's singing.*)

BOY. Kala meeya kala, baby
Kala meeya par
Kala meeya kala, danen
Ahno hooyoo-aahh
Kama pafya kala jah
Ano wayoh kame fra

Kal me *(kal me)* ala-lah
Kal me Kal me eneh eneh tah
Kal me *(kal me)* ala rah
You kan kal me eneh dayoh nai
Kal me

DAPHNE. He is so. What is the word. For when you need attention.

LIZA. I think I'll go shower...excuse me.

(**LIZA** *exits.*)

(**BOY** *continues to dance, much more sexily. She takes her hat off.*)

(**DAPHNE**'s *hand slides over to* **AUGUST**'s. *She tugs on it to make him watch too. He does. They eat.*)

(*Juice drips down* **BOY**'s *arm. She licks it off.*)

---

* Please see Music Use Note on Page 3.

BOY. Kava mee weth ki-ses, bebee
Kava mee weth lah-ah
Rohl mee'een tizahna seetsa
Neveh kete nah
H'mo shaka nadoh nowah
Kava-ah lah vzahla baaaaaahhhhh

(**DAPHNE** *looks at* **AUGUST**.)

DAPHNE. Shall we play a little?

AUGUST. *(re:* **LIZA***)* She's right there…

(**DAPHNE** *pouts.* **AUGUST** *gives in.*)

AUGUST. *(to* **DAPHNE***)* Stand up.

(*She does.*)

Walk over to her.

(*She does.*)

Touch her shoulder.

(*She does.*)

Kiss her neck.

(*She does.*)

Ask her what she wants.

DAPHNE. *(to* **BOY***) Ti thelis?* (*Translation:* "What do you want?")

BOY. *(touching* **DAPHNE***) Esena.* (*Translation:* "You.")

AUGUST. *(to* **DAPHNE***)* Kiss her mouth.

(**DAPHNE** *kisses* **BOY**. **BOY** *begins to take off her clothes.*)

(*gently, firmly) Ohi. Stamata.* (*Translation:* "No. Stop.")

(*A beat.* **BOY** *stops stripping.*)

Fee-yeh. ("Go.")

BOY. *Then katalaveno…* ("I don't understand…")

(*beat*)

(**BOY** *skulks off.*)

(DAPHNE turns the radio off and pours herself a glass of juice.)

DAPHNE. Far too early in the day for *that*.

AUGUST. Indeed.

(a beat)

DAPHNE. You say that word so much. "Indeed."

AUGUST. I never / noticed

DAPHNE. It is a way of shutting down.

AUGUST. A what?

DAPHNE. You affirm something indirectly, and therefore it ends the discussion. "Indeed." My father used that word all the time in English. It makes my fingers clench the air.

AUGUST. I won't say it again.

(DAPHNE sits.)

I've never seen you like this, *kota*. It's kind of thrilling.

(a beat)

DAPHNE. I want to ask you something *Avgusto* and I am not interested in the truth but it is important for me to say these words out loud so I have the memory of them hanging.

AUGUST. If you aren't interested in the truth, chicken, what do you expect me to say?

DAPHNE. Your closest approximation.

AUGUST. I'll do my best…

DAPHNE. I want to know if you will make love with that woman.

AUGUST. Will I make love to Liza. I wish I knew how to answer that.

DAPHNE. Try slowly, with feeling.

(a beat)

AUGUST. I want to say this: "No, Daphne. No I will not." I *want* to say it.

(a beat)

She isn't beautiful you know, traditionally. Her face is. Kind of saggy? She doesn't take care of herself. Not like you. And she's, she sort of reeks of damage, which is.

DAPHNE. Yes?

AUGUST. I don't know. You know when Liza, when she — You don't want to hear this.

DAPHNE. I very much do.

AUGUST. When she, she um climaxes...she cries. Every single time. I'm not talking little vanity tears, I'm talking these gasping terrifying sobs. First time it happened I thought I had hurt her. Because she kept asking me to go harder, harder. And then she's bawling, she can't breathe, and me "I'm sorry I'm so sorry" and. And she says, "It's not the pain. It's the mortality."

DAPHNE. I see. So making love to Liza is like making love to death. You are attracted to death.

AUGUST. No no, the opposite...there's this tiny little pea sized hunger spinning beneath it all...when you get *that* close to it, I mean — It's impossible to talk about.

DAPHNE. I see. And how does it feel to making love with me?

AUGUST. Making love with you. You.

DAPHNE. I.

AUGUST. You're very quiet, first of all. And delicate. I could shatter you.

DAPHNE. Oh.

AUGUST. And you take your time, none of the rushing urgency that. Um your fingers aren't clamps, they're feathers, and.

(beat)

You make me feel massive. Like a conquistador!

DAPHNE. You enjoy her more.

AUGUST. No no it's just / different

DAPHNE. Do you imagine her when we make love.

AUGUST. No. Sometimes.

DAPHNE. Oh.

AUGUST. I picture her hair greasy. You don't sweat, Daphne. Did you know this?

DAPHNE. I.

AUGUST. Ever. I've never seen you sweat.

DAPHNE. Oh.

AUGUST. I picture her sweating. I picture her nails cutting into my arms.

DAPHNE. Oh.

AUGUST. Not all the time, okay. Just when I feel a little. Ah lost.

DAPHNE. Oh.

AUGUST. So.

DAPHNE. Oh.

AUGUST. Are you. Okay?

DAPHNE. No.

AUGUST. Will you be?

DAPHNE. No.

(**DAPHNE** *picks up a knife from the table and stabs herself in the womb. She doubles over in pain, but a moment later, she rights herself as though nothing has happened.*)

(*A beat. They eat in silence.*)

I want to ask you something *Avgusto* and I am not interested in the truth but it is important for me to say these words out loud so I have the memory of them hanging.

AUGUST. If you aren't interested in the truth, chicken, what do you expect me to say?

DAPHNE. Your closest approximation.

AUGUST. I'll do my best...

DAPHNE. I want to know if you will make love with that woman.

AUGUST. Will I make love to Liza. No, Daphne. No I will not.

DAPHNE. Good. Because she breaks me.

(They continue to eat in silence. Lights down.)

(Time passes. It is late afternoon. The stage is soaked in November's melting Mediterranean light, buttery and lush and wicked.)

(DAPHNE enters, ecstatic. She carries a large fancy shopping bag.)

(LIZA and AUGUST follow happily.)

DAPHNE. Ah! That was precisely what I needed! My spirit is refreshed! Do you not feel this way, Liza?

LIZA. I do, Daphne. Like a weight has been lifted.

DAPHNE. Yes! And always after shopping I have a small hilarity in my throat when I return home and remove clothing from bags. I have obsession for texture, I think. Touching different leathers. This one is tough, this one is soft and wrinkled, this one is like glass...and simply nothing compares to the smell of something new...

LIZA. It's a great feeling...

(AUGUST cheerily pours himself a whisky.)

AUGUST. Whisky, / anyone

LIZA. Sure!

DAPHNE. It is affirming. I can phrase it no other way. Placing a new good thing on your body. In a manner it is saying, you are a good body. Liza, I must tell you again, I do not often accept gifts from people I do not know well. This holds a very warm place in me.

LIZA. Oh, / now

DAPHNE. I want to keep saying. Your generosity is was unexpected but and also unnecessary, and I feel very touched by it.

LIZA. Well you're cooking for me and everything, so.

DAPHNE. It does not to equal this. You are a gracious / woman

AUGUST. *(laughing)* Okay, enough! Are we getting a fashion show or what?

*(**DAPHNE** scampers away giddily. **AUGUST** hands **LIZA** a drink.)*

Well *that* was the quickest way to my wife's heart.

LIZA. You're welcome.

(They clink glasses and drink.)

AUGUST. I feel like I need an acid bath to burn that place off me. God the WASTE! And that FOUNTAIN! They need an enormous spouting pool of water when they have the ocean two miles down?

LIZA. Some European developer's wet dream. So to speak.

AUGUST. And that huge tacky Parthenon-ey facade…that alone probably cost a fortune. Goddamn it. If I had that kind of money I'd –

LIZA. You'd what.

AUGUST. I'd…seriously? How much are we talking.

LIZA. Millions. Many.

*(**AUGUST**, thinking.)*

AUGUST. Wow. Huh. Okay gimmie a second…This is now, right?

LIZA. Tomorrow, say.

AUGUST. Here?

LIZA. In the states. California.

AUGUST. Um. Okay. Who do we have on our side.

LIZA. The ACLU?

AUGUST. Perfect! So this is a me and you thing!

LIZA. Yeah. I'm the Ike to your Tina!

AUGUST. Love it. Great. What about Danny B.? You still talk to him?

LIZA. He moved to LA and planted a family.

AUGUST. Fuck. Well, we're loaded, right? We'll relocate them to the Bay area and get cranking on his old lobbyist contacts. Get a paid full-time staff. A REAL office. One with air conditioning this time. Mobilize a *full-scale* grass-roots lobbyist movement.

LIZA. *(triumphant)* That's him. That's my August.

AUGUST. *(deeply serious)* We'll bring that mother-fucking slimy-haired geriatric turkey-necked bible-thumping actor-cowboy down to his knobby arthritic knees.

LIZA. We sure as fucking hell will....

(**LIZA** *rushes to grab her purse, energized. She pulls out a beat-up, much-read paperback. The face of Ronald Reagan adorns the cover.*)

AUGUST. You saved this.

LIZA. Remember what you wrote inside?

AUGUST. "To My Lascivious Something. Suck on this. Love, Mega-Marx."

LIZA. No, in the margins.

(**AUGUST** *flips through the book.*)

AUGUST. My manifesto.

LIZA. Yup. And a game plan. For when we got to Berkeley. And some notes from our rallies, talking points and stuff....

AUGUST. *(reading, mountainous)* "There comes a time when the apparatus is so corrupt, so sickening, that you have no choice but to act. And you've got to seize the levers, take hold and scream at the edge of your voices to those who run it, scream that unless they hear you, the engine will be stalled."

Ha! Now *this* is something my kid could be proud of.

LIZA. You're right, he would.

(**LIZA** *approaches* **AUGUST** *warmly.*)

(**AUGUST** *closes the book and hands it back to her.*)

AUGUST. He'll be proud of the vineyard too.

(beat)

LIZA. The what?

AUGUST. You know most people equate *wine* with *wealth*. They see wine drinkers as like a *type*, going to tastings, getting – buying magazines...*Because.* They fall prey to an, to a hackneyed and patently Western notion of class identity. THAT is a travesty, in my opinion. Wine has the potential to be a true, a true populist...

(Searching. **LIZA** *gives him nothing.)*

And this country has so much potential. We're no longer under foreign governance, we're joining the EC next year, we elected a democratic president in May...who knows, in twenty to thirty years, Greece could become...

(Still searching.)

And I'll tell you something Liza, it feels so goddamn good be in on the ground level. I can actually *do* something. Build something with my bare hands. You can't build jack shit back home without piles of money. It's a dead country. No offense.

LIZA. You left the states so you could save Greece? Because I thought you blew your life savings on a beverage and had nowhere else to go.

AUGUST. That's not why we / left the states

LIZA. Because you found a woman who kinda STEAMS with priviledge, who just *happened* to come with a huge chunk of free land...

AUGUST. Well that's true –

LIZA. And now you're indulging a wine fetish and calling it activism. So, like, if I handed you a wad of cash right now, you'd what. Mobilize a grass-roots lobbyist movement in California? Or bury it in the dirt with those fucking grapes?

AUGUST. I –

LIZA. Who are you, August?

(beat)

*(***DAPHNE** *promenades into their view. She is wearing a gorgeous sparkly gown and high heels.)*

(Beat as they take her in. She is beyond stunning.)

AUGUST. *(amazed, quietly)* Daphne.

DAPHNE. *Voila!* I am a holiday!

*(**LIZA** applauds and hoots.)*

LIZA. Hoo, dang! Bravo! Bravo! August you are one lucky son of a bitch. ...

AUGUST. *Ehis klepsi to pneuma-mou...* *(Translation:* "You have stolen my breath..." *)*

DAPHNE. That is the most beautiful thing you have said to me...

LIZA. What did he say?

DAPHNE. He says I have stolen his breath...but the word *pneuma*, it also means spirit...I have stolen his spirit...

LIZA. Quite a dress!

DAPHNE. A designer from Paris. He is very famous. So famous no one can afford his clothing!

AUGUST. Liza. How much money did you spend on my wife today?

LIZA. What difference does it make.

AUGUST. I'd like to know.

LIZA. That doesn't answer my question at / all, August. What *difference* does it really make how much I spent on your wife, it's spent. Gone.

AUGUST. *(overlapping, slowly)* I'm not interested in answering your question, I'm interested in knowing how much money you spent on my wife.

LIZA. Twelve hundred dollars.

*(A beat. **DAPHNE** tries to maintain her poise, but she is ashamed.)*

AUGUST. Um.

LIZA. She fell in love with the dress. It looked delightful on her. She said she hadn't had a new dress in. Seven years, I think? I thought to myself, now THAT is an outrage. So I did what I could to help.

AUGUST. Could, ah. Someone please explain to me how this transaction occurred.

LIZA. What do / you mean

AUGUST. Step by step. Who said what, who asked / for what.

DAPHNE. You spent twice the cost on her last night.

(small beat)

I will take it / off

AUGUST. *(smoldering)* No no, don't bother. I'm sure it'll come in quite handy. We have a SLEW of functions coming up. Society balls, galas, et cetera. God forbid we show up looking like village trash. Speaking of, maybe you should show off your new wardrobe to your people down the way?

*(**DAPHNE** is quiet.)*

No people? Ah well. They'll come around.

*(to **LIZA**)*

Daphne doesn't get along with her people. She had an incident. Did you tell your new friend about the incident?

DAPHNE. *Avgusto.*

AUGUST. Daphne had an incident with / someone in the village.

DAPHNE. *Meen ise toso malakas.* (*Translation:* "Don't be such a bastard.")

*(confidentially, to **LIZA**)*

AUGUST. Daphne's particularly. It's very sweet, actually. *Sensitive* to beautiful things. And beautiful people. Better look out, next thing you know she'll have her tongue between your legs too.

(Beat. Immediate and genuine regret.)

Jesus. That was horrible. Fuck. I don't know what I'm thinking.

Excuse me.

*(**AUGUST** exits.)*

DAPHNE. He is unbearably touchy about money. Do not let it affect you.

LIZA. I didn't.

DAPHNE. Oh.

(small beat)

Well. It is good we celebrate today. Tomorrow shall be a day of mourning.

LIZA. Mourning? Why?

DAPHNE. The tasting. Oh Liza. His wine will not be good. It will be very sweet, very quick on the tongue. Very simple.

LIZA. What?

DAPHNE. The heat that harvest four years ago was exceptional and he picked his grapes too late. When the grapes are too ripe you get jam, not wine. He has no idea.

LIZA. Well he seems to know what he's doing, so…

DAPHNE. *Now* he does. His technique is improved.

LIZA. Still. There's no telling how it'll turn out.

DAPHNE. I have tasted it. Last week. Against his knowledge.

LIZA. …last night…

DAPHNE. I did not drink last night to show a point. Women must do the small dishonest things sometimes in order to retain our presence…You understand this.

LIZA. No uh, I only do big dishonest things…

*(**DAPHNE** smiles.)*

DAPHNE. I like you a good deal more than I did yesterday. And my dress looks fabulous on me. And tonight we shall have glamour and elation. And we shall make *Avgusto* with wearing the suit he was married to me. You will find him beautiful, Liza.

LIZA. I already do.

DAPHNE. MORE beautiful.

LIZA. Not possible.

DAPHNE. We are lucky women to be company with such a man…

LIZA. Indeed.

(a small beat)

DAPHNE. *Indeed.*

*(***BOY*** appears, smiling lopsidedly. She is very very drunk.* ***DAPHNE*** *grabs a shopping bag and approaches her.)*

Agapi-mou! Ela'tho. Sou efera thoro. (Translation: "My love! Come here. I have something for you." *)*

*(***BOY*** *approaches* ***DAPHNE****, smiling.* ***DAPHNE*** *opens a bag and pulls out a record.)*

Rotisa ton andra sto magazi yia "Blondie." Mou to edose afto… "Eat to the Beat." Simeni "Fa'eh sto rythmo." (Translation: "I asked the man in the shop for "Blondie." He gave that to me…"Eat to the Beat." It means "Eat to the Beat.""*)*

*(***DAPHNE*** *mimes eating to the beat.)*

*(***BOY*** *takes the record and strokes the cover. She glows with love, but then stumbles drunkenly and smashes into the table.)*

DAPHNE. *(laughing)* He is so drunk!

LIZA. Kids! What can ya do.

*(***BOY*** *gathers herself, then leans over to kiss* ***DAPHNE*** *on the mouth.* ***DAPHNE*** *turns her cheek to* ***BOY****.* ***BOY*** *receives a mouthful of hair.)*

*(***DAPHNE*** *glances at* ***LIZA*** *uncomfortably.)*

*(***BOY*** *is extremely hurt by this gesture. She hurls the record across the room.)*

Agapi! (Translation: "Love!" *)*

BOY. *(screaming) Yiati then me kitas san teen kitas? Yiati? (Translation:* "Why don't you look at me like you look at her?"*)*

DAPHNE. *Agapi… (Translation:* "Love…" *)*

(BOY begins to cry. DAPHNE goes to her and BOY tears herself away and lunges at LIZA, spitting at her. LIZA gasps.)

BOY.   DAPHNE.

Se miso! Fee'yeh, Fee'yeh!   *Ohi! Ohi! Ftani! Ohi!*

("I hate you! Leave!   ("No! No! Enough! No!")

Leave!")

(DAPHNE tears BOY off LIZA. BOY stumbles to the side and throws up.)

DAPHNE. *(cont.)* Oh…*agapi-mou*… *(Translation:* "Oh…my love…")

(DAPHNE grabs a tissue and cleans BOY's face.)

BOY. *Me pezees ke me pezees*… *(Translation:* "You play me and play me…")

DAPHNE. Shhh….

(DAPHNE strokes BOY's hair and rocks her. LIZA checks herself to make sure she isn't hurt.)

Please forgive him / Liza, he

LIZA. *(vicious)* What the fuck…

(a beat)

DAPHNE. Pardon?

LIZA. Are you messing around with her like she's some kind of a…a/

DAPHNE. This is not your concern, I am afraid.

LIZA. If you're abusing that child it's no longer a private matter.

DAPHNE. Some might call it giving pleasure.

LIZA. Does she look pleased?

DAPHNE. She is ill from too much drink.

LIZA. She is in LOVE with you.

DAPHNE. You truly find this tragic? Or are you having the classic American pre-occupation with morality?

LIZA. CHRIST, the self-indulgent, uh so-called love for beauty, you / are POISONING her!

DAPHNE. This is perfect Liza, the way your mouth opens and words tumble out and you have no filter for your brain

LIZA. And him! He used to be so, so HUGE, but now he's like a stump, and you're standing there like it's something to be proud of.

(A beat. **DAPHNE** *continues stroking* **BOY***'s hair.)*

DAPHNE. *(coolly)* Liza. Have I told you that I adore my dress?

LIZA. You have.

DAPHNE. I adore it so much that I shall continue to wear it regardless of the vulgar person who paid for it. And thank you for the sermon. Now I have tending to other matters. Excuse me.

*(***DAPHNE*** stumbles off with* **BOY***.)*

*(***LIZA*** stands. She walks around the space, a bit manic. She retrieves her bag from the corner of the porch.)*

(She reaches into her bag and pulls out a much-viewed photograph.)

*(***AUGUST*** emerges, looking beaten.)*

AUGUST. Where's Daphne?

LIZA. The um. The teenager had a bit of a meltdown.

*(***LIZA*** points to the corner where* **BOY** *threw up.* **AUGUST** *investigates.)*

AUGUST. Oh man. Sorry about that. He's at an awkward age. Hormones raging...no real family...

(small beat)

I hope you aren't hungry. Dinner could be a while –

LIZA. Your wine will be terrible.

(small beat)

AUGUST. Sorry, I didn't hear you.

LIZA. YOUR WINE WILL BE TERRIBLE.

AUGUST. I didn't hear you.

LIZA. It will – It will be terrible.

AUGUST. I'm not comprehending you.

LIZA. Your, your wine, it / won't be

AUGUST. *No comprende*

LIZA. It will be / ter, ter

AUGUST. I can't hear you.

LIZA. Ter, just bad, your wine

AUGUST. Sorry, what did you say?

    (small beat)

LIZA. Nothing.

AUGUST. You said / some

LIZA. I was talking to myself.

    *(Another long beat. **AUGUST** glances back toward the house.)*

AUGUST. I hope you aren't hungry. Dinner could be a while –

LIZA. I'm not hungry.

AUGUST. We'll eat like real Greeks, at midnight…

    (He rubs his head in exhaustion. She approaches him, hand outstretched. He backs away.)

Look, we're taking all that crap back to the store tomorrow, the / shoes, everything.

LIZA. I don't want her to take anything back. / They were gifts.

AUGUST. Liza. Why the. WHY would you ever EVER spend twelve hundred dollars on clothing for my wife.

LIZA. Because I can.

    (a beat)

I'm, I have. A lot.

    (a beat)

AUGUST. Of money.

LIZA. Yes.

AUGUST. When you say "a lot," I mean, / what are

LIZA. Sixty million dollars.

(Another beat. **AUGUST** *is floored.)*

AUGUST. Did you hit the fucking lottery, or…

LIZA. Not really.

AUGUST. Then…

LIZA. It's a bit of an anecdote, uh…a *legend,* actually…

AUGUST. An inheritance, what…?

LIZA. Kind of…

(a long expectant beat)

AUGUST. Are you gonna tell me?

LIZA. Um.

I think I should be holding you when I do.

*(***LIZA*** *approaches* **AUGUST** *and touches him gently.)*

AUGUST. Jesus. Listen, Liza. I have to ask you to leave. First thing in the morning. I'm sorry. It's just better. For everyone.

LIZA. I can't –

AUGUST. I am going to be a father in exactly twenty-five weeks and four days. I'm not going to blow this. I don't want to and I'm not going to. Do you understand?

LIZA. No.

AUGUST. Good.

(a beat)

*(***LIZA*** *hands the photograph to* **AUGUST.***)*

(She hands it to **AUGUST.***)*

AUGUST. What's this?

LIZA. Graduation from middle school. He just turned fourteen. It was raining.

(Suddenly, anything breakable in the vicinity shatters at once – frames, vases, glasses, potted plants.)

(Neither **LIZA** *nor* **AUGUST** *notice.)*

(long stare)

AUGUST. *(small voice)* What...

LIZA. I know. It's scary sometimes. And his laugh is exactly the same as yours too, that sardonic snort when he's feeling superior. And he's a terrible dancer. He talks in his sleep like you do. Um, what else...

AUGUST. *(quietly)* What are you showing me...

LIZA. And he. Doesn't cry.

(a beat)

He is a punched hole. He is a fallen leaf. He is made of light. He really is. Blue sparks in my mouth and yours when we made him, we were chewing and screwing in the dark because the sparks turned us on.

AUGUST. We made a boy.

LIZA. Out of light.

(a beat)

I will tell you the legend now.

AUGUST. Look at / him, my God

LIZA. My legend, August. It's my only legend...

(The air somehow changes...the lights melt...)

*(**BOY** appears, as a **BOY**. He is dressed in a graduation robe. He moves delicately, deliberately, much different than the slouchy street-urchin of earlier.)*

(He speaks softly, in a deep voice.)

BOY. July 28, 1978.

Your mouth is chomping wint-o-green after wint-o-green right now. You're in the kitchen surrounded by bills. I can hear you through the vents as I write this. You chew faster when you're anxious. Maybe you're chewing as you read this. Illegible. Crossed-out.

I know this is sloppy but I wanted to preserve each thought as it left my pen to give an accurate record of illegible. Crossed-out crossed-out scribble wanted to.

But first, business. You should sell anything that has some value, like my bike and my records and my books. Not my hi-fi. The left speaker is broken. I left my pot in the top drawer for you, but it's kind of old. Scribble scribble crossed-out forget it, that wasn't funny. My clothes are probably worthless, they were when we bought them.

BOY. *(cont.)* Now here's the crossed-out part. I know we said I'd try but illegible crossed-out illegible not changing, nothing changes and it won't. Like remember how I had that so-called break-through and I told Dr. Randy that the world felt fake, and that I was the only one who knew it was fake? I still feel this way, but it's much worse now because crossed-out scribble sorry, my knuckle hurts.

*(**BOY** moves his knuckle the way **AUGUST** did earlier.)*

But knowing this is not true and feeling it in my heart are two different things.

And I can't stop, I play every single scenario over and over in my head only it's worse now because I do it over really small things. "If I brush my teeth this morning, THIS will happen. If I don't, THIS will happen." Or like, "If I blink my left eye, THIS will happen. If I blink my right, THIS will." And then I think, if all the different outcomes for every single tiny thing are endless, how can ANYTHING be real? And then the ringing starts just like before and then I get weightless and I'm shaking and throwing up again. And the crossed-out panic doesn't ever illegible. Especially at night. My heart beats so hard my eyeballs bounce. It would be cool if it didn't make me illegible.

You just yawned really loud. It was funny. In a few seconds your head will be on the table, and you'll be drooling onto the phone bill. I'll touch your head on my way out, so maybe you'll still feel my hand there when you wake up.

BOY. *(cont.)* Oh, do you remember Colleen, the girl from the Y who used to write with her toes to impress people? You were right, I did have sex with her. But only once. She smelled like paper. I always felt bad about that lie.

Don't save this letter, okay Mom? Just read it once. Then burn it.

Love you,

August

*(**BOY** freezes somewhere on stage.)*

LIZA. I've heard that drowning is painless. You just have to fight the urge to breathe. But I guess he did that a long time ago, so. Um. A state-owned campground near Tahoe, there's this lake with this. Boat ramp. On either side of the ramp is a ledge with a sudden drop-off. When the water is high you can't see it. Two kids drowned in that exact spot the previous summer... Um he wanted to make it seem like an accident for my sake, so...

So a, a citizen's coalition had been trying to convince the state for years to erect a fence or a concrete barrier around the ramp, but they were roundly ignored...so this of course sent them in a tizzy. And the papers went nuts.

I, uh, filed a wrongful death suit. Got every penny I asked for. The publicity helped of course...I didn't talk to anyone, reporters, neighbors...When the cameras were around, which was like EVERY DAY for a while, I just. Hid my face with my hair.

Oh and I. Burned the note.

*(**BOY** disappears. A beat.)*

The ultimate screwing of the system, right?

(a long beat)

What, ah. What are you thinking?

AUGUST. I'm backing up in my brain to yesterday morning, before you got here, I'm trying to. See how I felt then because. Because I don't think I'll ever get that feeling back.

LIZA. He is the roots and we are the leaves. Now we have to rebuild from what he left us.

We're gonna use that sixty million and we're gonna bring that mother fucking actor cowboy down to his arthritic knees.

AUGUST. *(quietly)* I wasn't there for him….

LIZA. Come home, August. This is not you. You are a MOUNTAIN. Everything here…It's ersatz. It doesn't exist.

(She strokes him. He leans into her.)

AUGUST. …I *AM* home…

LIZA. No, August. I am your home.

AUGUST. I wish you had never come…I wish you weren't here now…I want you to leave and never ever think of me again, never come near me, or my wife, or my baby…

I hate you Liza…do you understand / these words…

LIZA. You hate yourself…

(He turns away. She stands, and slowly removes her shirt. She's in her bra.)

AUGUST. This isn't a game…

LIZA. I know…

AUGUST. Fucking pack your shit and leave…

(She bites him hard on the neck. He pushes her back begins tearing at her clothes viscously and kissing her everywhere. He is wild…)

You you you you you…

(After a bit, he begins to break down, bawling. They remain like that, sprawled across one another, clothes ripped, him crying on top of her. He rolls off.)

(After a moment, LIZA stands and removes her shoes.
She removes her jeans. She removes her bra and panties.
She leaves them in a pile on the floor. A beat.)

LIZA. I'm going for a walk, August. I am going to walk down
to your vines. I am going to lie down in the dirt. And I
will wait there for you. I will wait there until you come
to me. And if you never come, I will still wait.

(She exits.)

(AUGUST sits still a moment. He wipes the tears off his
face and clears his throat. He pours himself a whisky. He
sits back down in the chair and stares ahead for a while,
not drinking.)

(DAPHNE enters, still wearing her sparkly gown.)

DAPHNE. Well. Boy is passed out finally. Your friend I am
sure spoke of the incident...

AUGUST. Yeah...

DAPHNE. She is where?

AUGUST. She...went for a walk...

DAPHNE. Your rudeness to me gave her power. I do not
want to be in the same room with her again. She is
a troubled woman I understand, but she insults me
continually and I cannot remain dignity. *Retain.* Please
when she returns tell her to leave by tomorrow. I will
cook dinner tonight but she must find breakfast herself. I will eat in the kitchen if you must have her as
company out here...what is on your neck?

(DAPHNE approaches AUGUST.)

You're bleeding...how did...

(DAPHNE realizes these are teeth marks. She sees LIZA's
clothes heaped on the floor.)

No, *agapi...*

AUGUST. I need a moment, please.

DAPHNE. *(quietly furious)* Of course you do. And you have
been crying. This is all very emotional.

AUGUST. Please, Daphne, just give me a moment alone.

DAPHNE. Yes, you will get your moment alone, you will get many of them. This I would not have predicted. I thought more self-respect from you. No, naturally this happened, it is exactly right. You have a coward in you. It is your ugliest part. Could you not have held yourself? Are you so stinking with desire that you cannot smell what an animal she is?

AUGUST. You can think what you want, and I, at this moment. I can't help you.

DAPHNE. What do you mean?

AUGUST. Go.

DAPHNE. What do you mean? What do you mean?

AUGUST. Please. Go downstairs.

DAPHNE. I want to understand / what you have just told me...

AUGUST. (quietly) Go. Go.

DAPHNE. I will not...

(AUGUST smashes his whisky on the table, loudly. A beat.)

(DAPHNE quietly, and with dignity, exits.)

(AUGUST stares ahead a moment. His eyes soon shift to the pile of LIZA's clothes. He stands and approaches them. He picks them up and begins to walk toward the direction LIZA exited.)

(He stops, stares ahead. He returns to his seat, still holding her clothes. He drinks his whiskey. He does nothing.)

(Night falls, the stage darkens. AUGUST remains outside.)

(Morning. AUGUST's head is resting on the pile of LIZA's clothes. The bottle of whiskey is nearly empty.)

(AUGUST awakens. He rubs his eyes and his head. He looks around groggily. Birds chirp, a far-off rooster crows. It is morning. He has slept outside all night.)

(LIZA enters, still naked. Her back is covered in dirt.)

(a beat)

(He holds out her clothes to her. She takes them but does not dress immediately.)

LIZA. I. Couldn't keep waiting. I got cold.

AUGUST. Would you like a towel?

LIZA. No.

(a beat)

AUGUST. She'll be up any second.

LIZA. August, I want to hear you tell / me what you've

AUGUST. I just, I think it will be best if you have your clothes on when she comes up.

LIZA. Oh. Of course…

*(**LIZA** dresses.)*

*(**DAPHNE** enters in her robe and sees **LIZA** putting on her clothes.)*

DAPHNE. Well. You are both still here. *Avgusto,* my nerves are very slight. If you have made a decision, please invoke it and either spare me your faces or let us get on with our day.

(long beat)

*(**AUGUST** turns to **DAPHNE**.)*

AUGUST. I'm sorry.

DAPHNE. *(quietly furious)* That's it?

(beat)

Understand this. You will never know your child, *Avgusto.* You are a father who is dead.

(She hands him her wedding ring and exits. Beat.)

LIZA. Are you okay?

AUGUST. No.

LIZA. Will you be?

AUGUST. No.

*(**DAPHNE** returns.)*

DAPHNE. Well. You are both still here. *Avgusto,* my nerves are very slight. If you have made a decision, please invoke it and either spare me your faces or let us get on with our day.

(long beat)

(AUGUST *turns to* **LIZA.)**

AUGUST. I'm sorry.

LIZA. Okay, great.

(to **DAPHNE***)*

Lovely meeting you.

(LIZA *hands the Reagan book to* **AUGUST.)**

Guess I won't be needing this. But *you* might. In case you need to remind yourself of who you could be. If you weren't such a fucking coward.

(LIZA *exits. Beat.)*

DAPHNE. Are you okay?

AUGUST. No.

DAPHNE. Will you be?

AUGUST. No.

(DAPHNE *disappears.)*

(Long long beat. The air fills with sound.)

ANNOUNCER. In other news…things often burst.

(The sound builds.)

(BOY/AUGUST JR. *enters in cap and gown again, swigging from a bottle. He carries dirt.)*

(Slowly, **AUGUST** *approaches* **BOY.)**

End of Play

Also by
Sheila Callaghan...

Ayravana Flies, or A Pretty Dish

Crawl, Fade to White

Dead City

Fever/Dream

Roadkill Confidential

Scab

**That Pretty Pretty, or
The Rape Play**

We Are Not These Hands

Please visit our website **samuelfrench.com** for complete descriptions and licensing information.

OTHER TITLES AVAILABLE FROM SAMUEL FRENCH

DEAD CITY

Sheila Callaghan

Dramatic Comedy / 3m, 4f / Unit Set

It's June 16, 2004. Samantha Blossom, a chipper woman in her 40s, wakes up one June morning in her Upper East Side apartment to find her life being narrated over the airwaves of public radio. She discovers in the mail an envelope addressed to her husband from his lover, which spins her raw and untethered into an odyssey through the city...a day full of chance encounters, coincidences, a quick love affair, and a fixation on the mysterious Jewel Jupiter. Jewel, the young but damaged poet genius, eventually takes a shine to Samantha and brings her on a midnight tour of the meat-packing district which changes Samantha's life forever—or doesn't. This 90 minute comic drama is a modernized, gender-reversed, relocated, hyper-theatrical riff on the novel Ulysses, occurring exactly 100 years to the day after Joyce's jaunt through Dublin.

"Wonderful...Sheila Callaghan's pleasingly witty and theatrical new drama that is a love letter to New York masquerading as hate mail... [Callaghan] writes with a world-weary tone and has a poet's gift for economical description. The entire dead city comes alive..."
–The New York Times

"*Dead City*, Sheila Callaghan's riff on James Joyce's *Ulysses* is stylish, lyrical, fascinating, occasionally irritating, and eminently worthwhile...the kind of work that is thoroughly invigorating."
–Back Stage

SAMUEL FRENCH STAFF

Nate Collins
President

Ken Dingledine
Director of Operations,
Vice President

Bruce Lazarus
Executive Director,
General Counsel

Rita Maté
Director of Finance

ACCOUNTING

Lori Thimsen | Director of Licensing Compliance
Nehal Kumar | Senior Accounting Associate
Glenn Halcomb | Royalty Administration
Jessica Zheng | Accounts Receivable
Andy Lian | Accounts Payable
Charlie Sou | Accounting Associate
Joann Mannello | Orders Administrator

BUSINESS AFFAIRS

Caitlin Bartow | Assistant to the Executive Director

CORPORATE COMMUNICATIONS

Abbie Van Nostrand | Director of Corporate
Communications

CUSTOMER SERVICE AND LICENSING

Brad Lohrenz | Director of Licensing Development
Laura Lindson | Licensing Services Manager
Kim Rogers | Theatrical Specialist
Matthew Akers | Theatrical Specialist
Ashley Byrne | Theatrical Specialist
Jennifer Carter | Theatrical Specialist
Annette Storckman | Theatrical Specialist
Dyan Flores | Theatrical Specialist
Sarah Weber | Theatrical Specialist
Nicholas Dawson | Theatrical Specialist
David Kimple | Theatrical Specialist

EDITORIAL

Amy Rose Marsh | Literary Manager
Ben Coleman | Literary Associate

MARKETING

Ryan Pointer | Marketing Manager
Courtney Kochuba | Marketing Associate
Chris Kam | Marketing Associate

PUBLICATIONS AND PRODUCT DEVELOPMENT

Joe Ferreira | Product Development Manager
David Geer | Publications Manager
Charlyn Brea | Publications Associate
Tyler Mullen | Publications Associate
Derek P. Hassler | Musical Products Coordinator
Zachary Orts | Musical Materials Coordinator

OPERATIONS

Casey McLain | Operations Supervisor
Elizabeth Minski | Office Coordinator, Reception
Coryn Carson | Office Coordinator, Reception

SAMUEL FRENCH BOOKSHOP (LOS ANGELES)

Joyce Mehess | Bookstore Manager
Cory DeLair | Bookstore Buyer
Sonya Wallace | Bookstore Associate
Tim Coultas | Bookstore Associate
Alfred Contreras | Shipping & Receiving

LONDON OFFICE

Anne-Marie Ashman | Accounts Assistant
Felicity Barks | Rights & Contracts Associate
Steve Blacker | Bookshop Associate
David Bray | Customer Services Associate
Robert Cooke | Assistant Buyer
Stephanie Dawson | Amateur Licensing Associate
Simon Ellison | Retail Sales Manager
Robert Hamilton | Amateur Licensing Associate
Peter Langdon | Marketing Manager
Louise Mappley | Amateur Licensing Associate
James Nicolau | Despatch Associate
Martin Phillips | Librarian
Panos Panayi | Company Accountant
Zubayed Rahman | Despatch Associate
Steve Sanderson | Royalty Administration Supervisor
Douglas Schatz | Acting Executive Director
Roger Sheppard | I.T. Manager
Debbie Simmons | Licensing Sales Team Leader
Peter Smith | Amateur Licensing Associate
Garry Spratley | Customer Service Manager
David Webster | UK Operations Director
Sarah Wolf | Rights Director

GET THE NAME OF YOUR CAST AND CREW IN PRINT WITH SPECIAL EDITIONS!

Special Editions are a unique, fun way to commemorate your production and RAISE MONEY.

The Samuel French Special Edition is a customized script personalized to *your* production. Your cast and crew list, photos from your production and special thanks will all appear in a Samuel French Acting Edition alongside the original text of the play.

These Special Editions are powerful fundraising tools that can be sold in your lobby or throughout your community in advance.

These books have autograph pages that make them perfect for year book memories, or gifts for relatives unable to attend the show. Family and friends will cherish this one of a kind souvenier.

Everyone will want a copy of these beautiful, personalized scripts!

ORDER YOUR COPIES TODAY!
E-MAIL SPECIALEDITIONS@SAMUELFRENCH.COM
OR CALL US AT 1-866-598-8449!